Books by Niki Livingston

Theia's Moons Series
Eyes Wide Shut
Enyo's Warrior
Protectors of the Stars
Guardian

The Chaos Awakened Saga
Marked Chaos – coming August 2020
Expanded Chaos – coming November 2020
Transformed Chaos – coming February 2021

Novels
Be My Leprechaun

Novellas
Wrong Side of the Mirror

Novelettes
A Web Through Time
Wicked Heart
Wicked Soul
Jolly Old Monster
Unable to Wake

WRONG SIDE

OF THE

MIRROR

Don't get stuck looking out instead of in.

NIKI LIVINGSTON

Wrong Side of the Mirror

ISBN: 978-1-952537-02-8

Publisher: Unbound Wonders

Editor: Novel Nurse Editing

Cover Artist: Unbound Wonders

To connect: www.NikiLivingston.com

TABLE OF CONTENTS

To MaKayla Anne.

You saved me from my demons.

CHAPTER ONE
Lady In Red

It was only three nights at the Stanley Hotel. What could possibly go wrong?

I stared at my reflection in the gold-trimmed mirror, smoothing down the baby hairs of my shoulder-length maroon locks. I then shifted my gaze toward Ashley. "Ghosts don't scare me." I flashed her a tight smile, hiding my apprehension. "I'm in."

She clapped her hands and bounced off my bed, then threw her arms around me from behind. "What an adventure! And Jimmy will be excited that you're joining us." Her cocoa-brown eyes were filled with amusement as she looked at me through the mirror. "Maybe he will finally make his move."

I elbowed her with a glare. "No funny business, Ash."

She giggled and collapsed back on my bed.

I whirled around. "I'm going for the fun, not the boys."

"Then it will be the best time ever!" she exclaimed, falling back and throwing her arms above her head. "I need this, Issa." She rolled on to her side. "Thomas needs a break from his parents, and I need some time alone with him. Thank you for being a dear and putting up with my ghost adventures."

"No problem, hon." I turned back to the mirror and finished applying my mascara to my long, fake eyelashes.

I tugged on my black robe and pointed hat with purple trim, the finishing touches to my witch costume. "What time tomorrow are we leaving? It's only an hour drive from here." I reached down and grabbed Ashley's hand, then tugged her off my bed.

"We want to go on the night tour, and the main building is closing the next day for renovation and maintenance." She wrapped her arm around my waist as we left my room. "If we make it up there by five that evening, we should have plenty of time to eat and make the tour." Grabbing my shoulder, she turned toward me. "Your eyes look like sparkling emeralds with the makeup you have on. I like."

I grinned and bowed with prayer hands. "Thank you!" I turned my head slightly. "Bye, Mom!" I yelled down the hallway. "Don't wait up. I will be out late."

Mom's head popped out of her bedroom doorway. "Drive safe, you two." Her gaze skimmed over our costumes, and her brows raised slightly.

My witch dress only hit mid-thigh, but my robe was long, covering my knee-high boots and any leg I had been showing. I could still see the disapproval in Mom's eyes. Ash, as always, wore the most revealing costume she could find. Her version of Cleopatra would have the Egyptian gods striking us both down with their thunderous lightning the moment we stepped outside. The dress barely covered her ass, and the front scooped down so far that I swear one of her girls would pop out with little persuasion.

Ash skipped over to Mom and planted a kiss on her

cheek. "We are always safe. Don't worry about us."

Mom laughed. "It's not you two I'm worried about now." She shook her head and hugged Ash. "Those boys are in trouble tonight."

I grabbed Ashley's elbow and pulled her away. "Love you, Mom. We will be on our best behavior." I didn't look back. My mom was my favorite person on this planet, but I hated those judgmental looks.

"Love you more," I heard her call as I ushered Ashley out of the house.

"Your mom is so cute," Ashley gushed, throwing her arm around my shoulder.

I shot her a sideways look and shook my head. "She means well." I unlocked my car door and slid into the driver's seat, tucking in the top of my hat so it would not fall off.

The party was already raging when we arrived. Lighted lanterns in purple and orange adorned the walkway, and a giant skull floated against the frame of the house. Inside, a strobe light was flashing, and the silhouettes we could see from the car featured the partygoers mashing together as the lyrics to the song poured into the dark night.

Ashley shrieked. I whirled around, smacking the back of my head on the glass in the process, and saw a masked clown pressed against the passenger window. After throwing open her door, Ashley leapt out of the car and shoved the person.

He pulled off his mask. It was Thomas. "Your faces!" he whooped, doubling over with laughter and pointing at Ashley.

I rolled my eyes and kicked open my door. Jimmy stood a few feet away, sporting black jeans and shirt, with demon horns flanking the top of his head. His face was smeared with black and red face paint, along with a smirk that spoke volumes.

I threw him a smile and glanced at Ashley. "Not the best way to show your lady a good time," I said to Thomas.

Thomas wrapped his arms around Ashley and planted a kiss on her nose. "I'll protect you, my sweetcakes."

Ashley melted into his lanky build. Figures she would forgive him so quickly. I pushed past them and followed the lantern trail toward the house with Jimmy right behind me.

"It's great to see you, Carissa," he said, putting his hand on my shoulder. "Ashley really missed you while you were gone this summer."

I peeked in a window and then looked at Jimmy. "I missed her too. But I'll tell you what, leaving after high school graduation for a few months and seeing another part of this country was the best thing I have done for myself. New York was amazing."

He nodded. "I've been to Manhattan with my dad," he replied, scooting around me and opening the door.

The music blared in our faces, and I laughed from the vibration tickling my cheeks. Throwing my hands above my head, I jumped inside and crashed through the crowd, moving instinctively to the beat of the song. I really did need a night out, and then a few days in Estes Park would be perfect before I started my new job.

"Issa!" someone squealed a few feet away.

I turned and smiled at Dana, Thomas's sister. She was a year younger than us but was by far my favorite between the siblings. I rushed forward and threw my arms around her neck.

"Hey, beautiful lady!" I yelled in her ear. "It's so great to see your face."

"When did you get home?" she yelled back, holding on to my arms.

"A few days ago." I pulled back and grinned at her. "My mom has barely let me out of her sight, so this was my first chance to get out and see everyone. It's really good to see you, Dana. Are you coming to Estes Park with us tomorrow?"

Dana's face fell. "You're all going to Estes Park? Is my brother going?"

I sighed. There I went again, spilling the beans. "I believe so," I replied. I scanned the room, and found Ashley, Jimmy, and Thomas pouring drinks in the kitchen. "I bet he just hasn't gotten around to asking if you wanted to go." I smiled at Dana and grabbed her hand. "Let's go find out right now, because *I* want you

7

to come with."

I dragged her behind me through the crowd and tapped on Thomas's shoulder as I snuck around him. He looked at his sister.

"Hey, sis." He then bit into a cookie and turned back toward Ashley.

"I invited Dana to go with us to Estes Park tomorrow," I said from the other side of the counter.

Jimmy whipped around. "You're going with us?" he asked me as a bright smile lit up his face.

"Yes, she is." Ashley leaned over the counter and patted my hand. Her face tilted slightly to look at Thomas as she twirled her jet-black hair with one of her fingers. "And Dana is always invited on our adventures."

Thomas smirked at Ashley, then lifted his lips into a smile as he turned toward Dana. "Of course you're coming. I would never leave you here alone with our hammered parents."

Dana grinned and hugged Thomas. "I was worried there for a minute."

Phew! Turning my attention back toward the crowd, a dark-haired woman in a bright-red dress caught my eye. She stood nearly a head above most the crowd, making her stick out like a sore thumb. Her face was difficult to make out with the strobe light, but there was something off with her expression. I squinted to make out who she was as she stood still against the dancing crowd. Tuning out the others, I stepped around Thomas and Dana and shimmied through another group, doing my best to not lose sight of the woman.

As I neared her, I could see blood glistening on her cheek. The tiny droplets seeped from her eyes. I caught her gaze, and she tilted her head at me as I approached, smiling wide and revealing blackened teeth. I shifted around another dancer, and she flickered as if she were a hologram. Surprised, I stepped back quickly and bumped into a warm body.

I whirled around, coming face-to-face with a tall, blond fella. "Hey, careful there," he said, grabbing both my shoulders to steady me.

I put my hands up in front of me. "Sorry," I

mumbled. I looked back toward the woman, but she had vanished. "Did you see that woman with blood on her face?" I pointed in the direction she had been standing.

He peered over me and shook his head. "I see Jack with red paint smeared on his face." He turned and pointed. "And Mindy over there has fake blood on her pouty, beautiful vampire lips." He smiled and waved at the blonde cheerleader. "Is that who you're talking about?"

I groaned. "No. Thanks for humoring me." I pushed past him and stomped into the kitchen. I needed a drink of ice water. As I stepped up to Ashley, a cold breeze swept across the back of my neck, sending shivers down my spine. I looked over my shoulder as a crimson flash of light swept right through me, taking my breath away. I swayed slightly, a wave of vertigo blackening my vision for a brief moment.

Ashley's arms wrapped around my waist. "Already tipsy there, Issa?" She laughed and leaned me against the counter. "Do I need to be the designated driver tonight?"

I shook my head, confused. Was I hallucinating? "I'm fine, Ash. Just got a little lightheaded." I pushed away the uneasy feeling and forced a wide smile at my friends. An unexpected laugh bubbled up my throat, and a sudden giddiness swelled in my chest. "Who is in the mood for a game of beer pong?" I pointed outside at the unattended table on the porch. "Ashley just volunteered to be my designated driver, so it's me against one of you." I pointed at each of the other three.

Jimmy raised his hand, and I waved for him to follow me, sticking my tongue out at the others as I strolled by. "See you on the flip side, suckers."

CHAPTER TWO

Check-In

"Ow," I moaned from the backseat of Thomas's Toyota 4Runner. "Could you avoid the potholes, please?"

Ashley giggled and turned around in her seat. "Aren't you wishing *you* had been the designated driver last night?"

"Last night?" I grumbled, burying my face in my blanket. "I'm fairly certain I didn't make it home until the wee hours this morning. Whose idea was it to stay out so late?"

"*Yours*," Dana exclaimed with a chuckle. "Don't you remember begging us to go have breakfast around two this morning?"

"And why in the world would any of you listen to me?" I revealed one eye from underneath my blanket and glared at all of them.

Jimmy reached over Dana and patted my knee. "Who *doesn't* listen to you?"

"You're all mad." I shook my head as I pulled the blanket completely off. Leaning forward, I tapped Thomas on the shoulder. "Please tell me we are close. I have to pee."

"Twenty minutes tops," he replied, his ash-gray eyes meeting mine in the rearview mirror. "Can you hold it?"

"I guess." I exhaled in a huff as I sank back into my chair.

"Hey, grumpy pants." Ashley reached over and grabbed my knee. "Are you hangry or just hungover?"

My eyes narrowed slightly. "Both." My stomach gurgled loudly as if it was answering her too.

Ashley's gaze jumped from my face to my stomach and then back at my face. She grinned. "We will stop at the first fast food restaurant so you can pee and buy some food. Will that make you happy again?"

I nodded my head once and then stared out the window. I hated beer. And drinking period. What came over me last night? My eyes drooped and I let them shut, tuning out the others as they talked about the upcoming night tour at Stanley Hotel.

"Issa, time to eat." Dana nudged me with her elbow, and I peeked out from underneath my eyelashes.

I yawned and stretched my arms out above me, opening my eyes completely and staring out the window. A smile broke across my face. Pizza. My favorite. The sign read *The Village Pizza,* which was all the encouragement I needed to open my door and hop out barefoot. Dana crawled out after me and then I reached in and scooped up my tennis shoes and wallet.

My senses were assaulted when I opened the door. The smell was absolutely delightful. I skipped to the restrooms and was back to make my order before anyone missed me. They laughed at my sudden jovial mood.

"Food does that to me." I sipped on my large glass of Dr. Pepper. "And an empty bladder."

The pizza tasted like heaven. I shoved the first piece of the "*Luau Babe*"—pineapple, ham, and extra gooey cheese—into my mouth and bit off way more than I could chew. But I didn't care. I moaned with happiness and leaned back in my chair, taking the slice of pizza with me.

"You weren't kidding." Jimmy stared at me from across the table.

I tried not to laugh at his astonished expression, and I nearly choked on the pizza. I had to look away as tears sprang up in my eyes. I quickly chewed and swallowed, then resumed my staring contest with Jimmy.

"I never joke about food." I shoved the end of the pizza in my mouth again, not breaking eye contact with him.

His brows lifted slightly after a few moments of making googly eyes at me. He sipped on his soda, then lifted his slice of pizza off his plate. "I like what we are doing here. I feel very connected to you."

I burst into laughter and finally diverted my eyes.

"Glad you're back to your normal self," Ashley said, leaning against Thomas's shoulder. One of her legs was over his, and her left arm was wrapped around his, making it hard for him to eat. "Now we can drop off our bags in our room and go exploring before the tour."

Thomas set his pizza down on his plate. "Whatever you want, sweetcakes."

She looked up at him with a smile and he kissed the top of her head.

I finished three slices of pizza and two cups of soda before we climbed back into the car and drove the few blocks to the hotel. The white building rose before us, taking up several acres and not looking anything like the haunted hotel Ashley had described to me.

Thomas parked the car, and we all tumbled back out and grabbed our bags from the back before heading into the main building. A sign outside read: Closing For Maintenance Tomorrow October 31st.

I stopped at the top of the stairs and turned back to face the hedge maze. The mountains were speckled with autumn colors and I sighed from the sight. This is why I loved Colorado. I drew in a long breath and smiled. The air was chilly but refreshing as well. I could see why so many people drove up to this town to get some rest and relaxation. It was healing.

As I turned back around, a woman in a red dress caught my eye on the far end of the porch. My breath caught in my throat as I slowly rotated to look that way, terrified I would see the disappearing lady from last night. But no one was there.

My eyes narrowed at the empty space, then I shook my head and glanced all around, making sure there was no one else around wearing red. A few people sat at a table on the other side of the porch and two kids were running through the maze, but anyone else was too far away to be mistaken for a woman in red.

I scowled. I must be losing it.

Hurrying through the doors, I caught up to the others who were up at the check-in counter.

Jimmy's hands were tucked into his jean pockets, and he leaned over and nudged me with his arm. "Did you get lost?" His electric blue eyes met mine, and he must have noticed my frantic look as he twisted all around to face me. "Are you okay? It looks like you've seen a ghost."

"Maybe it's just this place." I smiled, trying to make light of my brain playing tricks on me. "Something about being here is spooky in itself."

He shrugged and flashed me a tight smile. "Doesn't seem too scary." His gaze swept across the room and back toward the old-fashioned car that was showcased near the front doors. "I thought you didn't believe in ghosts."

"I don't," I snapped, a little too harshly.

My tone surprised me as my eyes briefly closed. When I opened them again, I avoided Jimmy's eyes and the warmth that had crept up to my cheeks. He was just trying to help soothe my fears. I shook my head and moved up next to Ashley, then leaned my head on top of her shoulder.

A minute later Thomas dangled three keys in front of us. I grabbed one and followed after him, with Dana and Ashley on my heels. As we passed by the front doors on our way to our building, my gaze skimmed over the porch once more, but now it was completely empty.

Our room was cozy with two queen-size beds. I

hadn't thought about who was sleeping where until now, but Ashley and Thomas dumped their bags on the bed at the far end. I looked at Jimmy and Dana.

"I'll take the floor," Jimmy said, dropping his bag in the corner and sinking into the chair near the television.

Dana and I glanced at one another. "Guess it's you and me in this one," I told her. I set my bag on the floor and collapsed on top of the bed. "Can we take a nap before the tour?"

"You can do whatever you like, hot stuff," Ashley cooed from her bed where she was snuggled up to Thomas. "We, on the other hand, are going to explore."

I closed my eyes, shoving away the eerie feeling that someone, other than Jimmy, was watching me. "Have lots of fun. Wake me when it's time for the tour."

CHAPTER THREE

The Ghost Tour

The two cushioned chairs in the corner of the room where we would begin our tour were a nice touch. I sank onto one and blew a kiss at the others who were sitting with the crowd, waiting to be scared. I wasn't one to conform.

The tour guide burst through the glass doors at the back, with a wide grin on his pale face. His gaze briefly caught mine as he pranced to the front of the room.

"Good evening, everyone. My name is Zack and I will be your ghostly tour guide this evening," he said, greeting us with exuberant energy. He swept his wavy, sandy blonde hair out of his eyes. "Are you all ready for a fright?"

Thomas whistled and Ashley squealed with delight, while the rest of the crowd quietly cheered. My raised eyebrows gave my feelings away as the tour guide's attention drifted back toward me. Busted.

"What about you, miss?" he asked, stepping toward me.

His grin rose all the way to his moss green irises, which sparkled with delight. He really loved his job.

I returned his smile a little too enthusiastically. "Ghosts don't scare this little lady."

His smile faltered for a split second, but then he tilted his head and smiled even wider—if that were possible. "Tonight they just might." He winked at me, then turned back toward the other tourists and dove into a story about the hotel's past.

The founder of the hotel moved to Estes Park for his health, he told us. Interesting I was just thinking how healing the air was here.

Zack waved everyone forward, and I trailed after the group. Jimmy fell back to walk next to me.

"Can we start over?" He shot me a sideways look.

I reached over and patted him on the back. "Don't mind my mood swings. I was tired and a little creeped out by this place, but I'm over it now."

His face broke out in a smile, and I had to smother a laugh. He had apparently been more worried about my tone of voice than I realized. I stepped closer and linked arms with him. He tensed from my sudden touch and then quickly relaxed.

"If there are any ghosts, I expect you to have my back."

His eyes met mine. "It's possible I would just throw you over my shoulder and take off out of this place. Would that count as having your back?"

"Most definitely," I replied, patting his arm before leaning against it.

The tour of the concert hall was fascinating. After Zack finished telling us the history of the Stanley Hotel, he let us wander around the room and up onto the stage. I stood on the wooden stage and looked out into the small concert hall. I twirled around, smiling at Dana who was watching me from her seat on the edge of the stage.

A flash of red caught my eye again and my feet

skipped against the wood floor as I skidded to a halt. My heart hammered in my chest. Whipping around, I looked up at the balcony where I had seen the movement. It was too dark to see much of anything. I shuffled forward and squinted my eyes. There was definitely someone up there. I took two more steps closer until Ashley bounded to the edge of the balcony.

"Boo!" she yelled, her voice echoing off the high ceiling.

The shriek that burst from my lungs surprised me. I stumbled backward, falling to the ground with a thud. I pressed the palms of my hands into my eyes before ripping them away and glaring up at Ashley and Thomas.

"Not cool!" I bellowed.

They both burst into laughter, along with a few of the other patrons. Most others looked as shocked as I did, especially Zack who could not seem to understand why anyone would want to cause havoc on his tour. His stories were interesting, but Ashley and Thomas were only here to be a disturbance and obviously frighten me.

He beckoned for them to come back down the stairs. "We need to wrap this up and move on to the main building. You won't want to miss this."

I grumbled under my breath just as I was lifted off the ground and planted back on my feet. I whirled around. Jimmy stood behind me with an amused expression on his face.

"You think that was funny?" I asked, pointing at Ashley and Thomas as they strolled toward us.

"A little," he muttered, hanging his head with a smirk.

I pressed my lips together, suppressing a stupid laugh. It was not funny. Ashley wrapped me in her arms, and I buried my face in her neck as the damn laugh bubbled up my throat and trickled from my closed lips.

"You *are* laughing!" Ashley exclaimed, pulling away from me.

I glanced at Jimmy who was bent over his knees, trying so hard not to laugh, but when he saw my face, tears spilled from his eyes as his smothered laughter burst from his lips. And then I couldn't hold back any longer. I collapsed to the ground in a fit of laughter, rolled to my back, and stared up at the catwalk near the ceiling.

"We really need to keep moving," Zack stated, interrupting our meltdowns.

I nodded. Jimmy hovered over me with a lop-sided grin. "Do you need help getting back up?"

I raised my arm up to meet his, and just as he yanked me to my feet, I caught another streak of red move just above me. I gasped and held on to Jimmy for support as I searched the darkness above, but this time there was nothing there. These flashes were starting to grate on my nerves.

Jimmy moved around me and down the stage stairs before glancing back at me. "Are you coming?"

I vigorously nodded as I hurried down the stairs and raced after the rest of the group.

As we left the building, I looked back one last time. The lights illuminated every inch that I could see, except the stage. Squinting into the darkness, I swear I saw a figure standing center stage, but Jimmy pulled me forward just as another group of tourists swept passed me.

I slipped my hand into Jimmy's, needing his reassurance I was not losing my mind. Zack was talking about the old groundskeeper who he claimed haunts the lands surrounding the hotel. A gentleman who still takes it upon himself to ensure the guests are kept safe. Even though he was a ghost, a sense of relief slid over me. Maybe he would watch out for us during our spooky stay.

When we reached the main building, Zack took us in through the front doors. The old car near the doors was a centerpiece for everyone's cameras. I slid to the back of the group, inspecting the porch from my safe place. I could not shake the feeling that someone was watching me and it chilled me to the bones.

By the time we reached the grand staircase, I was ready to retreat to our room. This building gave me the creeps. I trailed behind the others, looking at the few portraits that adorned the walls of the staircase. Several of the eyes moved with me and when I noticed I was the only one left on the stairs, I raced up the rest of the steps and after the group.

"Where were you?" Dana asked, linking her arm with mine. Her smile lit up the whole room. "He is telling us about Room 217 from The Shining. This is my favorite part."

My heart was in my throat and I just shook my head at her, not wanting to ruin her mood. I pretended like I was listening to Zack. But my gaze kept wandering up the staircase that was only a foot from where I stood. Where did that lead?

A cold breeze swept passed me from behind. I looked over at Dana to see if she had noticed, but she was fully immersed in the story of the disaster that occurred in Room 217, while it was under renovation. That's when I noticed the yellow tape blocking the hallway to our right. And the large, gold-trimmed mirror hanging on the wall next to the corridor.

I squinted at it. The group was crowded near it as they took photos of Steven King's famous room, but there was a darker shadow that did not seem to belong.

27

Releasing Dana's arm, I stepped around another guest, tilting my head to the left to see the mirror better. Near the bottom of the mirror, a woman's barefoot appeared, then she pivoted and the bottom of a red dress flashed into my view for a brief second.

I gasped. A heavy-set man pushed passed me, blocking the mirror. I shifted around him, but tripped over something on the ground. My arms flailed out for something to hold and I could feel my cheeks flushing. I was such a klutz. As I steadied myself against the corner of the wall that lead through the yellow taped barrier, someone grabbed my arm and hauled me away from the corridor.

I glanced up and came face to face with Zack. A scowl washed down his expression, tightening his jaw.

"Time to wrap this up," he called out, never taking his eyes off me. "We are not supposed to be so close to this area while they are renovating. The liability on the hotel if someone were to get hurt, would be outrageous." He raised his brows and nodded his head toward the grand staircase.

I took the hint, not daring to look back at the mirror as I raced to catch up with Dana and Jimmy. But as I rounded the corner to retreat down the stairs, I noticed Zack still standing near the blocked off corridor with his hand reaching past the tape. He shivered, but never took his eyes off the darkened corridor.

CHAPTER FOUR

Ghost Stalker

"Happy Halloween!" Ashley exclaimed. I groaned and rolled over just as she bounced on my bed. "Wake up, sugar. We are leaving to have breakfast and coffee."

I shot up in bed and looked around at the others. "How long have you all been up?"

"Nearly an hour," Dana grumbled from her perch at the edge of the bed. "Ashley is an early bird. Did you know that?"

"How are we friends?" I looked at Ashley with raised brows. "Normal people our age sleep in. What is wrong with you?"

"That's why you love me." Ashley danced around the room, picking up everyone's mess as she went. "I am not boring enough to be normal."

I shook my head and grinned. She was right. "Give

me twenty minutes and I'll be ready. Where are we eating?"

"*The Egg & I*, right down the street," Ashley replied. She dug into her purse and pulled out her pink lip gloss. "Hurry up, Issa. I'm famished."

Jimmy walked out of the bathroom, just as I came around the corner. His face lit up when he saw me. "Sleeping Beauty is finally awake."

I danced around him and punched him playfully in the arm. "Arc you telling me I needed my beauty sleep?" I placed my palms against my chest and shot him a surprised look. "I'm hurt."

"No—no," he stuttered, lifting his hands in mock surrender. "That is definitely not what I'm saying."

Thomas snapped his towel out and it struck Jimmy on his leg. "Is that any way to treat a lady?"

Jimmy glared at his friend.

"Boys, boys." I stepped between them and held my hands out at both of them. "This damsel in distress can take care of herself."

Dana snickered, and Ashley flopped back onto her

bed. "Get ready already," Ashley whined. Her cocoa-colored irises widened expectantly when my gaze met hers. "It's my turn to be hangry." She stuck out her tongue.

"On it, Ash." I bolted into the bathroom and yanked on my jeans and sweater, then tugged on my knee-high boots.

As I stepped back through the door, Ashley shoved my wallet and jacket into my hands and pushed me out the door. "I have the best idea," she whispered in my ear. She wrapped her arm around my shoulder and pulled me even closer as we strolled down the hallway ahead of the others.

"And what's that?"

"Let's sneak into the main building tonight after the maintenance workers finish their shift." She was bubbling with excitement. Now I knew why she wanted to leave the room so badly. She wasn't hangry. She was conspiring and needed my approval.

I sighed happily. Despite her reckless behavior, Ashley kept me on my toes. You never knew what she had up her sleeve. "And what would we do once we were in there?" I asked, glancing over my shoulder at the other three.

"Anything we want. We could check out these ghosts everyone talks about." She pulled me outside and down the steps, hurrying so the others wouldn't hear us. "We could be ghost hunters for real." She nearly squealed the last sentence.

I rubbed my ear and threw her a dirty look.

"Sorry." A giggle burst from her lips, and she came to a sudden stop and whirled around, towing me alongside her. "Issa and I have a fantastic idea for tonight," she gushed to Dana and the boys. "I'll tell you all about it when we are in the car."

"Why not tell us now?" Thomas asked. He pulled his keys out from his pocket and dangled them above Ashley's head.

She grabbed at them and then glared at him when he held them higher. "*Because*," she hissed, "there are listening ears all over the place. I don't want to ruin the fun."

Jimmy and Dana moved around the lovers' quarrel and stood next to me.

"Should we be worried?" Dana asked, her concrete-gray eyes boring into my soul.

"You know Ash," I replied, my gaze traveling past Thomas and Ashley and locking onto a dark-haired woman with a red dress walking near the hedge maze. The hairs on the back of my neck prickled when a bitter-cold breeze swept through my hair. "You never know when you should bring holy water and mace."

As if the woman heard someone call her name, she came to an abrupt halt and looked around, but it seemed she wasn't paying any attention to those surrounding her. Her gaze lifted to the top windows of the main building, and she stood as still as a statue for several long seconds. My eyes narrowed. Then, without warning, she whirled around and stared right at me. She was the same woman from the Halloween party and the blood was still dripping from her eyes.

I jumped backward and screamed, dragging Dana with me before she let go of her grip on me. The heel of

34

my foot caught on something behind me, and I thrashed out my arms as I fell, but then magically there were arms around me. Jimmy was pulling me back to my feet.

Ashley grabbed my hand with both of hers as Jimmy steadied me. "Are you okay?"

My gaze flashed behind Ashley. I stared at the spot the woman had been, but now there were just other guests staring back at me. "Did you not see her?" My voice trembled, and I bit onto my bottom lip so I would not start crying.

"See who?" Ashley asked, glancing behind her.

I pressed the palm of my hand against my quivering lips and shook my head. "This can't be happening," I whispered to no one in particular. "Let's go eat." I tugged Ashley alongside me and the other three followed us, not one of them saying another word.

The drive to the restaurant was quiet for the first few minutes, then Ashley began filling everyone in on her plan to sneak into the hotel that night. Jimmy snorted and Dana groaned, glancing over at me. I could feel her eyes boring into me and I knew my expression was stony. I flashed a tight smile in Dana's direction, trying hard to forget that I was being stalked by an insane ghost.

How did this happen to me? I was the biggest ghost skeptic this world had met.

And how would I tell my friends?

CHAPTER FIVE

My Exorcism

"I'm not going," I snapped at Ashley. I had just filled her in about the ghost lady and was more irritated then ever by Ashley's insistence that we still trespass into the main building. "I don't know who I saw this morning, but for the first time in my life, I'm starting to believe in ghosts. And this one seemed to have attached herself to me back at the Halloween party."

"Why do you say that?" Ashley asked.

It was close to dinnertime, and she and I had walked to Starbucks so I could talk to her privately. The whole day was thrown off course from this morning's encounter, and I was ready to go home.

I raised my brows. "When do I ever drink beer? And right before I challenged Jimmy to that beer pong tournament, I saw the same woman."

"Are you sure it was the same—"

"Yes, I am sure," I snapped again, interrupting her. "I have felt off since then, and I can't stay here another night."

Ashley leaned back in her chair and looked out the window. "What if we performed an exorcism?" Her gaze drifted back toward me. "Hear me out." She held out her hand just when I was going to object. "If a ghost has attached itself to you, running back home won't solve your problem. It will just tag along for the ride." She sat up straight as if a lightbulb had gone off in her head. "We sneak into the main building tonight and perform an exorcism, banishing the entity from attaching to any of us. Then we can leave it here with all the other ghosts that haunt this place."

I slowly shook my head, wanting to disagree, but it actually sounded like a better plan than the one I had proposed. She was right. The ghost would just return home with me. That was the last thing I wanted.

"Okay, you win." I took a sip of my coffee and smiled over the brim of my paper mug. "You make some really great points."

"I know. It's because I'm a genius."

"Yes, you are," I muttered and took another sip of my hot coffee. The caffeine was helping me feel better as well. "We need to make sure we have everything that is needed for an exorcism. It would be nice if one of us was appointed a minister or saint or whatever they are called."

"A priest?" The corners of Ashley's lips quirked up with amusement.

"Yeah, that." I fluttered my hand above my head as if it were obvious I had meant a priest.

"We don't need one," she replied and finished her latte. "Let's head back. I want to shop for all the supplies we will need."

I tossed my empty coffee cup in the garbage and followed Ashley outside. The temperature had cooled significantly while we had been inside the shop. I shivered and pulled my jacket tighter around me. The Stanley Hotel seemed to hover in the air as we drew nearer, and chills ran up and down my spine from the sight. What had I gotten myself into?

***

My eyes were glued to the crack under the door. A light swept on by and then slowly faded away, along with the footsteps it had brought with it. I exhaled my held breath.

"That was a close one," Jimmy whispered from our hiding spot, in the closet that stored tables and chairs.

I elbowed him and lifted my finger to my lips. He nodded his head in response, then zipped and locked his lips and threw his pretend key over his shoulder. A smile broke across my face. He was a lot more fun than I realized. And he had saved me more than once on our little ghost adventure.

Convincing the other three to perform an exorcism had been laughable. Jimmy and Dana had said no, at first, while Thomas agreed to do whatever Ashley wanted. Honestly, I think he was just excited to ditch the three of us afterward and find a quiet room for the two of them to be alone.

My gaze flitted back to Jimmy. His eyes lit up when mine met his and he reached over and tucked a wisp of my hair behind my ear. He had been worried about my ghost experience and his gentlemanly behavior softened my heart. Just enough to consider planting a kiss on his lips after this was all said and done. When I told him and Dana that this is what I needed for my own sanity, they both relented.

And now we were too far in to our secret mission to turn back.

Ashley and Dana were crouched in front of me with Thomas and Jimmy to my sides. Our bag of contraband was slung over my back. It was my exorcism so I had been saddled with the load of candles, salt, holy water—which Ashley had blessed herself—a black onyx crystal, and a holy cross. I hoped that was all we needed. Once it was done, I was leaving back to the room with or without the rest of them. Ashley was on her own for her ghost hunt.

Twenty minutes later, Ashley edged the door open a

few inches and peeked into the room. It was quiet and dark. We followed her out, one by one, tiptoeing to the old billiards room. Ashley had insisted it would be the best room for the exorcism. I was just happy it was close to the front doors.

My gaze flashed up the grand staircase, and I paused for a brief second. The moon shone through the window, casting shadows across the walls that were littered with old photographs and eerie mirrors. I shivered and raced after the others.

Ashley was waiting in the billiards room. She pulled the bag off my shoulder and dumped everything on the floor in front of the fireplace. After scooping up three of the candles, she walked a few feet out and placed one down, followed by the next a few feet away. As she was setting down the third candle, her gaze shot to the rest of us who were watching her in a state of awe and confusion.

"Are you going to help or not?" she hissed, standing up straight and folding her arms over her chest.

We all jumped into action. I snatched up four candles

and followed her direction, placing them in a circle around us. Dana put the largest candle in the middle of the circle, while the boys poured salt around the candles.

"How are we going to clean this up?" Jimmy asked. His gaze flitted over the mess we had made and then settled on Ashley.

Her left brow raised slightly. "I'm sure there's a vacuum around here somewhere."

He sighed, and I rolled my eyes. We were royally screwed if we were caught. They would consider it vandalism the way it looked right now.

Moments later, we were all sitting inside the salt-and-candle circle with me in the middle, holding the black onyx candle and crystal. Ashley reached out and set the wooden cross against my legs. Turning toward Thomas, she held out her hand and after he took it, she did the same with Jimmy.

"Now you two take Dana's hands," she ordered, nodding her head toward the younger girl. When Ashley was satisfied with the setup, she closed her eyes and drew in several deep breaths. "Oh, Lord God, mighty warrior of our souls, please crush the spirit that has taken refuge in Carissa's vessel. Banish this spirit from ever entering or attaching onto another living soul. Send your valiant angels and messengers to cleanse all our auras of this traumatizing event, and push to have this spirit enter the light so she will finally be at peace. With your majestic powers I entrust this task unto you. It is done. It is done. It is done. Amen." Her eyes flitted open and she glanced around at all our wide-eyed stares.

"Have you been anointed a monk or a priest or something?" Thomas asked, laughing at his own question. "Super sexy, by the way."

Ashley ignored him and turned toward me. "Did you feel anything? Did you see the woman again?"

I shook my head and set the crystal in my lap. "Maybe we should have hired a real priest."

"No way. I've got this." Ashley scooped up the cross and pressed it against my forehead. "Be gone, wicked spirit. In the name of our Lord God. Amen."

An intense shock shot through my body and I jolted forward, nearly knocking foreheads with Ashley. "What the hell was that?" I stammered, my gaze shooting around the room.

A chilled breeze swept into the room, and the doors that led to the front lobby slammed shut. Dana screamed, and I jumped to my feet. Jimmy leapt up beside me, wrapping his arm protectively around my waist. He tugged Dana off the floor and pulled her in close as well. My heart drummed inside my chest as terror slid through my veins like ice-cold water. Ashley and Thomas rose slowly and peered around the room, then moved in closer toward the rest of us.

We stood in a circle, our breath visible from the cold. It was deathly quiet, but after a few moments the chill in the air finally dissipated.

"I'm sure it was nothing," Thomas finally said, interrupting my racing thoughts. He stepped over to the windows at the far end of the room. "I say we finish this séance and then go explore the rest of the rooms."

"This is not a séance," Ashley and I both snapped at the same time.

He waved his hand in dismissal. "Whatever it is, let's

wrap it up. We have free reign of this castle for the night, and I want to see what the fuss is all about." After whirling back around, he hurried toward the lobby and pulled open the doors. "See, nothing to worry about. There must be an open window somewhere. I need to use the restroom, so I'll check it out on my way there." He pointed at the flickering candles. "You might want to put those out and clean up the mess as best you can."

Without another word, he jogged toward the grand staircase, disappearing around the corner before anyone could open their mouth to stop him. I fell to my knees and blew out the candles near me. Dana did the same, while Jimmy swept up the salt as best he could into his hands. Ashley stood as still as a statue, still watching the empty doorway Thomas had been standing in a moment before.

I set the candles just outside the doorway. "We need to let those cool before I put them back in my bag." I stopped in front of Ashley and cupped her chin with my hand. "He will be fine. Help us finish cleaning, and we can follow after."

She nodded. "Did it work, Issa?" Her worried gaze finally met mine.

"I don't know. I felt something, but then the doors slammed, and from there—"

"Then it worked," she said with a curt nod. She whirled around and stomped toward the salt, leaning over to help Dana and Jimmy sweep it up.

A shifting dark shadow caught my attention in the corner of my eye. I gulped and twisted my head to look just outside the billiards room. Something or someone was moving on the other side of the grand piano.

CHAPTER SIX

Separated

"Guys." I waved at them erratically.

They ignored me.

"*Hey*," I hissed.

Jimmy looked over his shoulder at me. I pointed at the front windows of the lobby, unable to move my feet. He was by my side two seconds later.

"There's someone on the other side of the piano," I whispered in his ear before pushing him in that direction.

Planting his feet in place, he glanced at me and then back at the piano. "Thomas, is that you?" he loudly whispered. He strained to see over the piano without moving forward.

"Did you see Thomas?" Ashley was suddenly standing next to me with Dana right behind her.

"Someone," I whispered, pointing.

Ashley pushed past both me and Jimmy. "Thomas," she barked, running into the middle of the room. "This isn't fun—" She froze and backed toward the front doors. "Who are you?"

My blood ran cold. Dana's hand gripped my own, and Jimmy yanked us both into the lobby and toward Ashley. Somehow, I dared to look back at the piano.

The dark-haired woman flickered like the candle's flame, but next to her was what chilled me to the bones. A grotesquely disfigured man stood hunched over with black orbs as eyes. Dana turned to see what I was looking at and stumbled backward, before whipping around and tearing up the grand staircase.

"*Dana, come back!*" Jimmy yelled, running after her.

Ashley and I hugged each other, backing all the way to the front doors. I pushed on the doors, just as I turned and came face-to-face with another man on the other side of the window, except half his face was missing, revealing stark white bones as his left cheek and eye socket.

A shriek bubbled up my throat and I pressed my fist against my lips, yanking Ashley toward the grand staircase. She screamed at the sight of the man. After ripping away from my grip, she raced behind the staircase, heading for the lower level where Thomas had gone to use the restroom. I stood petrified and unsure of which way I should run. Everyone had left me.

Reasoning with myself that Ashley would be easiest to find, I sprinted after her, tearing down the staircase. I rounded the corner at a full run, barreling full speed into Thomas and knocking both of us down. I slid across the floor and smacked my head against the wall.

"*Ouch*," I cried, rubbing the side of my head.

Thomas groaned and rolled to his knees. "What in God's name are you doing, Issa?"

I looked at him in shock. "Where's Ashley?" I gulped down the terror rising in my throat.

He leapt to his feet. "What do you mean, where's Ashley? She was with you when I left for the bathroom." He leaned down and hauled me up beside him.

"She ran after you a few minutes ago." I rose onto

my toes and looked over his shoulder. "It's so dark down here. How can you see anything?"

"My phone flashlight." He raised his phone, a dim light shining from it. "Just bright enough to see where I'm going."

"We need to find Ashley and the others." I pushed past him, walking toward the creepy white dollhouse I had seen during our tour the night before. "I watched Ash run this way. She couldn't have gone far."

"Maybe she went outside," he said, racing down the hallway toward the outside door. "The door we came through for the tour, it's over here."

Duh. I knew that. Losing sight of him, I picked up the speed and sprinted after him.

He came to a sudden halt in front of the door and cursed under his breath. "There must be an alarm on." He pointed at the red light next to the door. "She didn't go out this door, and if we open it we will trigger the alarm."

Whipping around, he nearly toppled right over me. I groaned and pushed him away. "Watch it, buster. And try not to lose me. I don't want to be alone when those demon ghosts show up again."

His eyebrows mashed together. "What?"

Shit. I forgot he wasn't there. Shaking my head, I pointed back the way we came. "Upstairs. We ran into three of them, including my favorite lady ghost. That's why everyone took off."

"You can't be serious? Ghosts don't exist."

I threw my hands up in the air and stomped back toward the stairs. "Fine, don't believe me. I really don't care. Let's just find Ash already."

As I passed by the dollhouse again, something out of place caught my attention. I stepped back and peered behind it. A figure was huddled in the corner.

"Ash?" I stepped over the rope barrier. "It's Carissa and Thomas."

Her head shot up, and she burst into my arms. Her entire body was shaking. Thomas leapt over the rope and pulled Ashley into a tight embrace.

"What the hell happened up there?" he hissed at me.

"I told you," I hissed back. "We need to find Dana

and Jimmy, now."

He didn't say anything, but when I darted back toward the stairs, I could hear him and Ashley right behind me. As we rounded the corner to go back to the front lobby, my heart sank into my stomach. *She* was right there. Waiting. She knew I would come back.

Her arm lifted and pointed up the grand staircase. I tiptoed forward and peered up the stairs. The moon was now shining straight through the window, lighting everything in its path.

"What the hell is that?" Thomas yelled.

I whirled around. He was dragging Ashley back the way they came, all the while staring wide-eyed at the dark-haired woman.

"Come on, Thomas." I waved him forward. "Don't you dare leave me. Your sister is up these stairs."

He stopped moving, his gaze flashing between me and the ghost. Twisting Ashley around to look at him, he put both hands on her cheeks. "Baby, wrap your arms around me and close your eyes. We have to find Dana and Jimmy."

Ashley didn't hesitate. Her arms wrapped tightly around his neck, and he swung her up in his arms. Not waiting for them to follow, I bounded up the stairs two at a time. A black figure stepped out from the corner, surprising me. I thrashed my arms out and nearly toppled back down the stairs until I felt someone's hand grab mine and pull me back up.

Those sparkling blue eyes met mine. "*Jimmy!*" I exclaimed, throwing my arms around his neck and kissed him hard on the lips. Breaking the kiss, I squeezed him tighter. "Where's Dana?"

"I can't find her," he muttered, either flustered from my kiss or the ghosts at the bottom of the stairs. His eyes snapped down to look at the entity still standing with her arm raised.

Thomas growled. "Which direction did she go?"

Jimmy lifted his head and arm, pointing up the stairs and to the right. After giving the ghost one last look, Thomas tore up the stairs and set Ashley down at the top. He waved at us to follow. Then he edged his way down the hallway, towing Ashley behind him.

I stole another look at the ghost, but she was gone. My heart pounded ferociously against my ribs. "Let's go." I grabbed Jimmy's hand and pulled him up the stairs with me.

CHAPTER SEVEN
Looking Out Instead of In

The hallway was dark, but I could make out the silhouettes of Thomas and Ashley not too far ahead. I crept forward with Jimmy right on my heels. There were strange dark shadows along the walls and as my eyes adjusted, I noticed the large gold-trimmed mirror we had walked by during the ghost tour, at the end of the hallway. I squinted at it. Something was wrong. I took a few quick steps closer and gasped, scrambling back against Jimmy's warm body.

He wrapped his hand around my arm and steadied me. "What's wrong?" he whispered right next to my ear.

I pointed at the mirror. "What is behind Thomas and Ashley?"

Jimmy moved around me and squinted. Then his eyes widened. "*Thomas*," he hissed, pulling me closer to his side.

Thomas stopped in his tracks and glanced over his shoulder. Jimmy pointed. Whirling back around, Thomas nearly jumped out of his skin. He picked up Ashley and pressed them both against the wall. His gaze flashed from the mirror and back to the space right behind them.

A gaping black eye socket on his half skeleton exposed face seemed to bore into my soul as the tall apparition stood motionless in the mirror. Terror thundered through every vein in my body. Clinging tighter to Jimmy's arm, I nodded at Ashley to come back toward me. She vigorously shook her head. Her eyes moved back to the mirror, and without a word, she dropped to her knees and crawled furiously toward the mirror.

"What is she doing?" I muttered. My fingernails were digging into Jimmy's arm.

He winced and looked down at me, before prying my hands from his arm. "We have to stop—"

Ashley's ear-piercing scream nearly brought me to

my knees. I stepped toward her, then stopped and looked at the ghostly man in the mirror. I was right behind him. Then my gaze caught another figure crouched in front of Ashley.

Dana.

I bolted forward, ignoring the chill as I rushed past the area the ghost was standing and joined Ashley at the foot of the mirror. Dana was staring back at us, tears streaming down her face. Her body shook with fear. I pressed my palm against the mirror, willing my hand to go through and pull her out, but the barrier held firm.

Thomas knelt between me and Ashley, pushing us both out of the way. "Dana?" he whispered. "No. No. This can't be happening." He glanced at Ashley and then at me. "What did you two do?"

"Nothing," I stammered, crawling back a few feet. "This was not us."

The temperature around me dropped, and Thomas's eyes widened as his gaze rose. "*Stay away from my sister!*" he screamed, jumping to his feet. He whirled around but then sputtered and grabbed frantically at the air in front of his face as he rose a few inches off the ground.

Ashley screamed and leapt to her feet. "He's choking him," she cried, struggling to catch her breath. Her hands pressed against her chest, taking several steps backward down the other hallway.

Jimmy and I grabbed Thomas around the waist and pulled him as hard as we could. A sinister laugh echoed around us as Dana pounded her fists against the other side of the mirror. Then Thomas dropped, and we all landed in a heap on the floor. My head snapped up. Ashley was gone.

"*No!*" I screamed, shoving Thomas's legs off mine. I scrambled to my feet, then stopped as something else caught my eye in the mirror. I slowly twisted around and collapsed back to my knees, sobbing as I fell against the mirror. "*Please, God, no.*"

A teary-eyed Ashley stood next to Dana with her arms around the other girl's shoulders. Thomas punched the wall next to the mirror, leaving a slight dent. He moaned slightly, cradling his fist in the crook of his other arm.

"How do we get you out of there?" I asked Dana and Ashley.

They both started talking at the same time, but I couldn't hear what they were saying. I pointed at my ear and shook my head. Their shoulders sagged and a look of dread and defeat flashed across Ashley's expression.

Jimmy stood silent next to the hallway Ashley had been standing in a few minutes ago. "Can you feel the chill in the air?" he finally asked. He twisted to look at me and Thomas. "There is something here."

I shivered. Thomas moved to stand next to Jimmy and reached out his hand, then nodded.

"This is why the hotel staff closed this building. Did you notice on our tour how the guide wouldn't let us come too close to this mirror?" Thomas whirled around and stared at me. "They didn't want the public to know they had a problem they couldn't fix. At least, not right away."

"What now?" I asked, not caring why they did it.

"I go in after the girls," he replied. His gaze traveled

around the area and then he ran to the stairs. "We need a rope or sheets. Something for you two to hold on to from this end. I can tie it around my waist."

"Have you lost your mind?" Jimmy asked.

Thomas glared at his friend. "My sister and girlfriend are stuck in that place with some creepy entity, who just tried to kill me. What do you want me to do? Let them rot in there?"

A light flickered at the other end of the hallway leading back to the grand staircase. A sob bubbled up my throat as it flickered again, but now it was closer. I recognized the dark hair of the ghostly woman.

CHAPTER EIGHT
The Other Side

"She's coming," I whispered, pointing down the hallway. "Whatever we are going to do, we need to do it now."

Thomas and Jimmy followed my gaze, then Thomas pivoted on his heel and flew up the stairs, leaving us to face the wretched entity. She grinned, flickering out right after. I released my held breath and glanced expectantly at Jimmy. One of us had to do something.

It was deathly quiet, and the only sounds I could hear were Jimmy's panicked short breaths and my pulse drumming in my skull. I looked at the mirror again. The tall man was back. He stood silently behind Ashley and Dana who were huddled together. But the entity was glaring at the hallway where the dark-haired woman had just been.

Both of his hands flashed forward, his fingers wrapping around Ashley and Dana's shoulders. And then they were all gone.

I whimpered, falling once again to my knees. "Please don't hurt them." I reached for the mirror, just as a hand patted the top of my head.

"Hold on to this," Thomas demanded, dangling the end of white linen in front of me.

I gripped the end, and Thomas tied another sheet to the other end of the one I was holding. Less than a minute later, he had tied together eight sheets and was wrapping the last one around his waist.

His eyes bored into me. "Do *not* let go."

"Never." I rose to my feet and wrapped the sheet around my right hand, then held it firmly with my left. "Jimmy, once he goes in, you will have to help me hold this."

A figure raced up to the mirror and a silently screaming Dana pounded at it. Tears streamed endlessly from her eyes. I couldn't stand to see her this way as my own tears tumbled down my cheeks. She was terrified, and there was nothing I could do but wait.

"Hurry, Thomas." My gaze met his. "Please save them both."

"I will." He stepped past Jimmy and walked down the hallway, then disappeared.

"Jimmy," I whispered.

He glanced my way. The sheets tightened, and I was suddenly tugged forward.

"Help me, please."

His fingers wrapped around the sheet just in front of me. We were pulled forward another few inches and Dana was still alone, weeping at the base of the mirror.

She stopped crying as her eyes widened and she pointed, screaming what looked like, *ghost*.

My head whipped to the side, loosening my grip on the sheet as I stumbled toward the mirror. The dark-haired woman stood inches from us. For the first time, I could see the features of her face. The blood wasn't dripping from her eyes. Instead there were two lacerations right below her eyes and another across her right cheek. She looked at me, then back at Dana, before flickering out again.

Jimmy gulped and stole a glance back at me. "Are you okay?"

"No, I'm not," I muttered. I gripped tighter onto the sheet and looked back at Dana. "She's in there with Dana."

Jimmy's head whipped around to look at Dana. The woman stood to the side of Dana, but she was pulling at something we couldn't see. Then Thomas came into view, and then the woman floated away from them, continuing down the hallway. She turned back around at the end and screamed, "*Go!*" before disappearing completely.

Thomas gathered Dana into his arms. He said something to her and Dana shook her head, pointing in the direction the woman had gone. Thomas turned toward the spot the woman had been, but Dana grabbed his arm and pulled him back, vigorously shaking her head.

I wished I could hear what they were saying. I tugged on the sheet, and Thomas looked at us through the mirror. He mouthed *Ashley* and then shook his head.

I choked back fresh tears. "He has to save her."

Jimmy looked back at me.

"Jimmy, she's my best friend. He can't leave her in there."

"I'm sure he will do whatever he can."

Thomas had undone the sheet from his waist and was tying it around Dana's. He waved at us. Dana reached out her hand to him just as we pulled on the linen. Then Thomas raced down the hallway and disappeared around the corner.

We pulled until Dana came stumbling back into view. I yanked her into my arms and held her as she sobbed in the crook of my neck.

"Thomas went after Ashley," she cried, pushing away from me. "The man took her. He won't let her go, and I'm so scared he will kill Thomas."

"Jimmy, I'm going in for them." I held up the end of the sheet rope.

"Just wait, Issa." His hands were balled into fists, and frustration crinkled the edges of his eyes. "Give him some time to find her."

My eyes narrowed and I started to shake my head.

"Good God, Carissa, we can't lose you too. Please just stay put." He blocked my view of the haunted portal hallway.

I puffed out my cheeks and exhaled in defeat. Exhaustion had spread to every muscle in my body, and I just wanted this night to end. I turned toward the mirror and waited. It was so quiet, I could have heard a pin drop.

My heart skipped a beat when Ashley tore around the corner, racing toward me, with Thomas not far behind her.

"Now. We have to go now." I fumbled with the sheet, trying to wrap it around me.

Jimmy snatched it from me and tied it around his waist. "You two hold on tight." He nodded at the end of the sheet rope.

"Wait, Jimmy. Stop." I held out my hand, but he was already through the portal.

Dana was already white-knuckling the end of the

sheet. I stood in front of her and wrapped my fingers around the fabric just as it tightened and yanked us forward. Tripping from the sudden movement, I face-planted onto the floor. Ignoring my bruised cheek, I leapt back to my feet. Dana was inching forward, unable to stop herself as Jimmy's weight pulled on the rope. I wrapped my arms around the girl and gripped the sheet, pulling back with everything I had.

Then the rope went slack and Jimmy stumbled back through, pulling Ashley with him.

I tugged her close, brushing her obsidian hair out of her face. "Don't ever do that to me again."

She sobbed and wrapped her arms tight around my torso. "Thomas stayed back. The woman—that scary-looking woman—saved me and now he says he has to save her." Pressing her face against my shoulder, her entire body shook as she wept uncontrollably.

"We are leaving," Jimmy barked, dragging Dana and me by the arms.

"We can't leave Thomas." I yanked my arm free.

Jimmy stepped closer. "He told me to get you three

out of here and then come back for him. Now get your ass moving, Issa."

"Ashley?" I turned to look at my friend.

"He did tell Jimmy to get us out of here." Her voice was barely a whisper.

I nodded and pulled her to my side. "Then let's go."

Prying open a window on the bottom floor was our best option. After our night of terror, we were overjoyed to find one that was already cracked. One by one, we scooted over the ledge and crept through the brush and back toward our room. Just as I stepped on the first stair outside our building, I noticed an older man standing near the main building in old-fashioned clothing. He tipped his hat at me and then disappeared around the corner.

I stared after him for a moment. Was he the one who cracked the window? As I was turning to follow the others, another figure tore around the same corner, racing toward us at top speed. Tears sprang to my eyes. It was Thomas.

CHAPTER NINE

"Should we tell someone?" Dana asked from the corner of the bench at *The Egg & I*.

My head snapped up from being pressed against the cool table. "What in the world would we tell them? And then the hotel might press charges against us for trespassing and destruction of property."

Jimmy piped up next to me. "Not to mention, breaking and entering."

Thomas had barely said a word since he ran into Ashley's arms only a few hours earlier. We had packed our bags and drove the car over to *The Egg & I* parking lot, where we all dozed off for a couple of hours. No one wanted to be in that hotel.

"Let's keep this to ourselves," Thomas said. He reached over and clasped Dana's hand. "We can't even tell Mom and Dad."

"Pfft." She rolled her eyes. "Like I ever tell them anything. They are the reason I came on this terrifying adventure with you." Thomas squeezed her hand a little too hard, and Dana winced. "Okay, fine. I won't breathe a word to anyone."

"Good girl." Thomas leaned the other way and wrapped Ashley in his arms.

She was zoned out and instinctively nuzzled into Thomas's chest. He seemed pleased with her touch in a way I had never seen before. Almost as if she was a possession that he had to protect from all others. He met my gaze and the edges of his lips twitched up with amusement.

"You never told us how you escaped," I said to Thomas. Propping my elbows up on the table, I then rested my chin in my hands. "Just something about the woman and her helping you back through. But how is that possible? She isn't tangible."

A frown melted down his expression. "I don't know how she did it, *Carissa*." He enunciated my name with a hint of malice in his tone. "One minute we were on one side of the portal, and the next thing I know, we were standing on the living side." He then smiled as if forgetting all about me and lifted his gaze to the ceiling. "And what a glorious feeling to be with the living once again." His eyes twinkled.

Jimmy and I glanced at one another and then at Dana. She was in her own world and hadn't noticed Thomas's strange behavior. Even his tone didn't sound right.

My gaze flitted to Ashley's, but her eyes were closed. She was not doing well, and I didn't blame her.

"Well, I don't know about all of you, but once we have eaten, I just want to get home and forget any of this ever happened. And hopefully my lady ghost friend will stay put with her creepy comrades up at the hotel." I leaned back in my chair and patted Jimmy's leg.

He smiled at me and wrapped my hand in his.

"I don't think you'll have any more issues with that ghost." Thomas's cynical laugh surprised me, but he didn't notice my raised brows as he stared out the window. "She will want to stay as far away from me—I mean our group as possible. Especially after the adventure we just put her through." He pursed his lips and started whistling an unnerving and sullen tune, sending goosebumps up and down my arms.

Jimmy nudged me. I glanced over as the color drained from his cheeks. Something was definitely off with Thomas. And the whistling did not end until the server brought us our food.

We ate in silence.

The drive home was so quiet, aside from Thomas's occasional whistling, that I finally shoved my ear buds in my ears and tuned out the eeriness with some *Lindsey Stirling* violin performances.

I stumbled into my house and locked the door. Mom was already at work. After a quick shower, I wrapped myself up in sweats and a blanket and melted into my bed. That was the worst Halloween in all my life. I rolled to my side and picked up my phone. A text message glared back at me.

Thomas: *Ashley wants nothing to do with you from here on out. She is mine now. Do not come around. This is your only warning.*

I stared at the text in disbelief. He had to be playing one of his dumb jokes.

Me: *Stop being a butthole, Thomas. Get some sleep and I'll talk to all you tomorrow.*

Thomas: *She is mine. Stay away.*

I shot up in my bed. How did Thomas really escape that portal? Or did he?

CHAPTER TEN
Scene of the Crime

The Stanley Hotel loomed above me. The front porch was mere yards from where I stood, but my feet would not budge. I had told myself I would never return, but Thomas and Ashley had disappeared and I needed answers. I reached over and entwined my fingers with Jimmy's.

"Why are we here, Issa?" he asked me again for probably the umpteenth time.

My gaze drifted over to his as my other hand curled into a fist to stop it from shaking. "Do you promise to stay here with me after I tell you? No matter what?"

"I have answered yes a hundred times now. Why are you being so secretive about this?"

"It is Thomas," I whispered, biting down on my quivering lip.

Jimmy pulled me in close to him, wrapping his arm around my shoulders. "Why are you shaking? Is this where Thomas and Ashley have gone?"

I never told him about the text message Thomas sent me. I vigorously shook my head against his chest. "No, I think Thomas never left. The Thomas we drove home with was not the same man who arrived to Estes with us. I swear it."

Jimmy pulled away from me, staring hard into my eyes.

I held up my hand to stop him from arguing, then rested it on his chest. "Now that they have disappeared, I have no doubts that something changed when he was inside that mirror. Please just humor me. We have to return to the mirror tonight."

"No way, Issa," he said, stepping away from me. A look of terror slid across his expression. "I can't go back there."

"But their renovations are complete," I replied, pointing at the front doors. "We can stay in the main building tonight and be normal guests in the hallways. I made sure our room was not far from the mirror."

A haunted look washed down his face. "You tricked me, Carissa. You told me we were not going inside the hotel."

I threw my hands in the air. "What if Thomas is stuck inside that mirror?"

Jimmy stood quiet for a few minutes, staring off at the Rocky Mountains. Then he heavily sighed. "Okay. I'm not convinced, but for you, I will do it. One question. If they found a way to close that portal, how will we find out if he is in there?"

I pulled on the strap of my backpack. "I brought a new black candle and all the other items as well. We find a way to see inside and then if Thomas is still in there, we do anything we can to free him."

"Are you telling me you think a ghost tore Thomas from his body and possessed it? Are you really going that far?" The line between his brows deepened as he frowned at me.

"You four all walked through a supernatural portal," I muttered, trying hard to hide my irritation. "And now you are questioning if my idea is going too far? I would have thought your disbelief in all that is ghostly would have been shattered after what we went through."

His gaze shifted to the main building, then over to the building we had stayed in only a few weeks earlier. I wrapped my arms around my torso, shivering from the chill in the air. The temperature had dropped significantly since our last visit and it was pushing me to go inside. But Jimmy needed more time to filter through his fears. I had the past week to come to terms with revisiting and now I was asking him to do the same in a matter of a few minutes. I knew the anguish he was feeling inside.

"What if you're wrong?" he asked, still looking at the far off building.

"But what if I'm right? Are you willing to take that chance on Thomas's life?"

He shook his head, then wiped at his eyes before turning back to face me. "Let's go then."

I took a hesitant step forward, before reaching back and grabbing Jimmy's hand again. Together we stepped up onto the white porch, then through the front doors, ignoring the piano and billboard room to our right. I just kept walking until we reached the check-in counter.

"I have a reservation under Carissa Allen," I told the lady behind the counter.

She nodded and clicked the keys on the keyboard, her long fingernails making it louder than normal.

"Yes, Carissa Allen. There you are." Her eyes narrowed for a split second, then she glanced up at me. "Have you been here before?" She pinned me with her eyes.

My stomach knotted into a ball. "It has been a while, but yes. Is there a problem?"

"No, not at all. We had an incident a few weeks back and one of the guests involved resembles you. We have been trying to reach the man who checked them in, but he is not returning our calls." She shrugged her shoulders and handed me the keys with a wide smile. "But it couldn't be you. The hair is completely different."

My lips quirked up slightly as I took the keys.

"Do you need help with your bags?" she asked.

I shook my head. "It is only for one night. I think we can manage." Turning toward the grand staircase, I nearly tripped over my own feet when I saw Zack standing over by the showcased car speaking to a group of tourists. I whirled back around. "Can you tell me where our room is?"

Her expression fell. She wanted to see how well I knew the hotel.

"Yes, of course." She pulled out a map. "Head up the grand staircase and take the left stairs to the second floor. Take a right. At the end of the corridor take another right. Your room is the second one to the left." She circled it on the map, then handed me the piece of paper.

I shot her a tight smile before hurrying off with Jimmy in tow. "It is a good thing I cut and colored my hair before we came," I whispered in his ear when we began climbing the grand staircase. "I stuck out like a sore thumb with my maroon hair."

The coffee brown pixie-cut hair was not my style, but

I knew it would be well worth it if I decided to go through with this plan.

As we reached the landing, I stared at the nearest mirror. A flashback from the night of the exorcism blew through my mind. The moon illuminating the mirrors as we searched for Dana and the unmistakable sensation that someone was watching me. It was unnerving even now.

I flew up the stairs, only stopping when we rounded the corner. Unable to stop myself, I turned back for one last quick look, when a freezing cold breeze smacked me in the face. Then a flash of red whisked past one of the mirrors. My blood ran cold. Was that my imagination or could I already reach the other side?

"I don't know if I can do this," I whispered, sagging against the wall behind me.

Jimmy's hand found mine. "I know what you mean, but we are here now. Let's finish this."

I nodded, forcing myself to turn toward the gold-trimmed mirror at the end of the hallway. We both walked slowly and despite the cold, my hands were clammy. I dropped Jimmy's hand and wiped my palms on my shirt, never taking my eyes off the mirror. As we approached, the only two figures I could see were mine and Jimmy's and I let out a lungful of air, relief washing over me. I was not ready to meet another ghost.

"Boo," someone yelled in my ear.

I toppled to the side, yelping as I smacked into Jimmy and nearly face planted into the red carpet.

CHAPTER ELEVEN

Trapped In the Mirror

"I am so sorry," I heard him say.

I steadied myself against the wall, then whirled around to see an angry Jimmy and an amused Zack.

"Are you following us?" I asked, glaring at the overzealous tour guide.

He held his arms up in the air as if he was surrendering. "I was just wondering why you two are back here so soon. We have cameras, you know."

I glanced at Jimmy. This was a horrible idea.

"I won't breathe a word," Zack said, interrupting my thoughts of escape. "I just want to know why you returned."

"Our friend—" I started to say, but Jimmy cleared his throat and stopped me.

"Our last visit did not go as planned," Jimmy replied, stepping in between me and Zack. "We are just here to make up for the ridiculous experience we had then. You understand, right bro?"

Zack glanced over Jimmy's shoulder at me, then he nodded. "Yes, of course. But I suggest you keep your head's down and maybe next time ask for the other building. The new hairdo doesn't help that much."

I reached up and ran my fingers through my short hair as he walked away. Jimmy watched him disappear down the stairs, then turned to face me.

"We cannot bring him into our circle," he hissed, clearly frustrated with me. "No more lives need to be impacted by those ghosts."

"Maybe he could have helped," I hissed back.

I stomped around the corner and down to our room, shoving the key into the slider. When we entered the room, the quiet wrapped tightly around us both. It felt safer inside these walls. I collapsed onto the bed and tossed my backpack to the floor.

"I'm sorry," I whispered, picking at my fingernails and avoiding Jimmy's eyes. "I can't imagine what Ashley must be going through right now and the thought of Thomas stuck in the mirror makes me sick to my stomach."

Jimmy knelt in front of me and wrapped my hands in his, kissing them one at a time. "This place brings out the worst in us, doesn't it?"

I nodded.

"We are in this together," he said, setting my hands back on my lap and crawling on the bed with me. He pulled me into his arms and laid back on the pillows. "I am with you every step of the way and when this is over, we are never returning to this town again. Deal?"

"Deal," I replied, snuggling into his chest. "Thank you."

Closing my eyes, I imagined we were in the Bahamas and this was just a dream. My body relaxed and Jimmy's breathing lengthened. We settled into one another, if for just a moment pretending we were not about to open a portal to the terrors of the other side.

I rolled over to my side and stared at the darkened window. The sun had set. We must have fallen asleep. I nudged Jimmy and then scooted to the edge of the bed.

"Is it time to get up already," Jimmy moaned, rolling to his side and snuggling into the pillow.

I laughed. "Get up lazy bones. We have a séance or exorcism or whatever to do."

He hauled his legs over the edge of the bed and sat up, rubbing his fingers over his whiskers. "How long did we sleep? I'm starving."

I fumbled in my backpack for my phone. "8:08. We slept for over two hours. Good thing, because we will probably be up late."

Sighing heavily, he rose to his feet and shuffled to the bathroom, shutting the door without a word. I pulled out the black candle, along with the eight white candles, situating them on the table near the window. Then I plopped the container of salt and holy water next to them. This time I found a real priest to bless the water as well as the tiny stone cross I had purchased at a thrift store. We had everything we needed.

Jimmy came out of the bathroom with a smile. "Let's order food. We can order pizza or just get room service. Your call."

"Pizza," I replied, setting a lighter next to the candles. "Pepperoni or pineapple and ham."

"Pepperoni it is."

He turned on his phone and looked for a pizza joint that delivered. A few minutes later he had ordered and we sat down on the edge of the bed, watching the muted television show. My gaze drifted around the room, landing on the gold-trimmed mirror above the dresser.

"We should try to reach Thomas right here," I murmured, saying the words before I thought them through.

"In our room?" he asked, a hint of fear laced within his tone. "This is where we will be sleeping. I would rather *not* invite the supernatural in."

I twisted to face Jimmy. "I don't think we will be getting much sleep tonight. Let's do it now."

"But the pizza." He pointed at the door as a look of desperation swept across his expression.

I was already arranging the candles in a circle in the small area between the bed and the table. Within a few minutes, the salt had been poured and all the candles were lit. I waved at Jimmy.

"We can sit in the middle together with the black candle between us."

I pocketed the smooth cross, then sprinkled us both

with the holy water. Jimmy's raised brows stopped me before I sprinkled the water inside the circle.

"You can't be too careful," I said, shrugging my shoulders.

"I thought you weren't religious. Where did you get your hands on holy water?"

I closed the container of water and set it back on the table. "The priest didn't know he was blessing it. I asked him to tell me the blessing for a college project and hid the vial of water in my hands."

He shook his head and chuckled as he sat cross-legged inside the circle of candles. I did the same, lighting the black candle in between us. Reaching out my hands, Jimmy grasped them with his and we rested our arms on our knees.

"I'm not as good as Ashley, but here goes," I said, then drew in a deep breath as I closed my eyes. "In the name of God, we ask that you surround us with your light and protection. Please bring forth our friend, Thomas, from his confinement within the mirror and free him from this prison. In exchange, return the entity who has stolen Thomas's body. Blessed be. And so it is."

My eyes flickered open and I looked at Jimmy, then up at the mirror. There was no one there. Jimmy patted my hand, then rose to his feet, hauling me up beside him.

"It was a long shot," he said, stepping closer to the mirror. "We will have to wait until we can sneak over to the mirror in the hallway."

I sighed, then picked up the black candle and blew it out. Jimmy jumped back. My gaze shot up. A face was pressed against the mirror, then they stepped back and Thomas came into view. His silent screams sent chills racing down my spine. I leapt forward and pressed my hand against the mirror just as he disappeared.

The phone rang. Jimmy shouted out in fear and I fell to the ground, digging my nails into the carpet to push out the screams in my head.

CHAPTER TWELVE
Black Tourmaline

"Our pizza is on its way up," Jimmy whispered after setting down the phone receiver.

I nodded against my knees. My arms were wrapped around my legs with my head hiding between my kneecaps.

"He is really in there." Jimmy sank to the floor next to me. His clammy hand found mine and he squeezed it. "You were right, Issa. Over three weeks he has been stuck in there and I didn't even realize it."

Someone knocked on our door. My head shot up as Jimmy fumbled back to his feet. A few seconds later he returned with the pizza and dropped it on the table.

"Are you hungry?" he asked, opening the box.

"Not really." I had to think. How would we bring Thomas out of the mirror? "What if we open this portal and someone else falls through to the other side?"

Jimmy was nibbling on the end of a slice of pizza. "It's a chance we have to take. We need to prepare to bring everyone back through if we have to. There are extra sheets in the closet."

I yanked at the strap of my backpack, pulling it closer to me. Opening it up, I pulled out the twenty foot rope I had brought with me.

"No need for sheets this time," I said, holding the rope up. "I came prepared."

"Brilliant." He picked up the rope and threw it on the bed, then pulled me up into an embrace. "We will get Thomas out of there."

I glanced at the mirror again, wishing Thomas would reappear. "We could do it again. Maybe this next time it will be stronger and the portal will open up in here."

"Or the portal will open in the corridor and we will be hauling people out of there all night long," he replied, shaking his head as he pulled away. "Or the hotel staff is forced to move everyone from their rooms and we lose the chance to save him. We need to play this safe.

It is after nine now. We need to wait until one, at least."

I followed him over to the table and picked up a slice of pizza as I stared out the window. It was going to be a long night.

***

My eyes were heavy, but I could not peel them away from the mirror. About midnight Jimmy fell asleep. I, on the other hand, was too nervous to close my eyes or take the chance of missing Thomas. I leaned my head against the bedframe. It was nearly one in the morning and almost time to wake Jimmy.

My phone buzzed. Reaching over to the nightstand, I squinted at the screen, then pulled it closer to my face. It was a text from Dana.

Dana: *Are you awake? You need to call me right now.*

I pressed on her number. It rang once and then she picked up.

"Issa, where are you?" she asked, her tone frantic.

"Jimmy and I are in Estes Park," I whispered, turning away from Jimmy. "What's wrong?"

"Thomas called." She lowered her voice.

My heart leapt into my throat. "He did? Where is Ashley? Is he bringing her home?"

"Issa, he's on his way to the Stanley Hotel," Dana replied. "He's furious. Says you are trying to hurt him. Wanted to know if I knew where you were."

Sweat trickled down my spine. I swung my feet over the edge of the bed. "He's coming here?" I glanced at the mirror again.

"I have never heard him that angry before, Issa. What are you doing?"

"We are saving your brother, Dana. How far away is he from Estes?" I leaned back and shook Jimmy.

"Maybe an hour. Probably less," she replied. "Why are you back there?"

Jimmy rolled over and looked at me with one open eye. "Is it time?"

I nodded, gathering the candles in my arms. "I can't get into the details right now, Dana, but I promise I will tell you more tomorrow." I set the phone down and ended the call, then shot a look in Jimmy's direction. "The wrong Thomas knows we are here. He's on his way right now."

Jimmy shot to his feet. "Was that Dana?"

"Yes. He called her looking for me. Dana said he is furious."

"Of course he is." Jimmy tucked the rope under his arm, then grabbed the lighter. "We are about to ruin his new life."

I opened the door and peeked out. The lights in the corridor had been dimmed and no one was around. A wave of déjà vu swept over me like an ice cold blanket. I signaled the all clear to Jimmy as I stepped out of the room.

We set the candles in a circle again, with the black one in the middle. As I lit the last one, a face appeared in the mirror. I gulped and stepped back. It was the lady in red; the ghost I had brought to the hotel.

She pointed behind us. I whirled around and nearly screamed when Zack shifted out of the shadows.

"I knew you two were up to something," he whispered, staring at the lady in the mirror. "Do you realize how long it took for us to close that portal? Obviously, we need to find a way to lock it as well. I have to report this. Looks like you two will be staying the rest of the night in jail." He pivoted on his heel, but Jimmy grabbed his arm, stopping him in his tracks.

"Just wait," Jimmy hissed, squeezing Zack's arm. "Our friend is trapped inside these mirrors and we are not leaving until he is freed."

Zack glanced at me, then at the woman in the mirror again. "Is that your friend? She doesn't seem to be the sort of person you want roaming around freely."

Thomas stepped up beside the woman and pressed his hand against the glass.

I choked back a sob. "No, that's our friend," I said, pointing at Thomas.

Zack's jaw dropped. "How did that happen?"

"We don't know," Jimmy replied, walking over to my side. "But the entity who stole his body is on his way back here as we speak. We need to figure out how to reverse whatever he did and return Thomas to his body."

"I know how to do it." Zack sighed, as he closed in on the mirror. He kicked away my candles. "You won't need those. And you don't need the portal completely open." His worried eyes scanned over the mirror and then the corridor that led to our room. "Have you experienced any cold drafts nearby?"

"Earlier, when we first arrived," I said, jabbing my thumb over my shoulder, toward the grand staircase.

He glanced back and stared for a moment, then nodded and pressed his finger against his lips. "We have to be quiet," he whispered, pulling out an object from his pocket. He set it in front of the mirror.

A black rock.

"How will that help?" Jimmy asked, his voice so quiet I barely understood him.

"Black tourmaline," Zack said, his eyes focused on the mirror. "It will prevent any negative entity from materializing on this side of the mirror or staying for that matter. It does allow all others through, but they are locked from escaping the area between the rocks." He dug into his other pocket and pulled out another one, then jogged to the grand staircase, setting the rock on the other end.

Thomas still stood silent on the other side of the mirror, watching Zack as he returned to us. I pressed my hand against the glass and he did the same. The lady in red watched with a sullen expression on her face. She didn't belong here either.

"Do you know who the ghosts are?" I asked, looking at Zack as he wiped beads of sweat from his forehead.

He glanced at the lady in red. "Not her. She is new. But the others have been here for years and every so often a guest figures out how to open the portal to the other side." He rolled his shoulders back as if he was about to start a fight. "There are a few of us who are constantly monitoring for signs of this. It's exhausting at times, but we are compensated well. We can't lose business."

I had brought the lady in red with me. When did she attach herself to me? I stared at her and she seemed to be thinking the same thoughts as she tilted her head toward me. Thomas tapped on the glass.

New York. He mouthed, pointing at the woman beside him. Then his eyes widened as they shifted to look behind me and he slammed his palm against the mirror.

A chill prickled up my spine as I spun around, coming face to face with the large, hunched-back entity from the night of the exorcism. His black orbs stared blankly at me.

CHAPTER THIRTEEN
Joining the Living

My fingers reached for Jimmy's, yanking him next to me as my fist pressed against my lips to squash the scream thrashing against my tongue. Zack looked at the entity and shook his head, before sinking to the floor.

"He's harmless," Zack said. Reaching up, he wrapped his hand around a gray rock hanging from his neck. "But you don't want him to attach to you. He's a nuisance and is always looking for an unknowing soul to hitch a ride with out of the hotel. The black tourmaline will keep him confined, but I suggest you stay close to me. The staurolyte will also protect us." He held up the rock in his hands.

The disfigured entity floated passed us, twisting his face toward me before manifesting on the other side of the mirror. Thomas cringed as he stepped away from the glass, allowing the ghost to continue down the corridor on his side of the mirror. The lady in red smiled as he passed, revealing her blackened teeth, and clearly unafraid of the apparition.

Thomas watched him disappear around the corner and then released a silent sigh. He turned back to the mirror.

Hurry, he mouthed.

His expression saddened and his gaze fell to his left hand. He lifted it for me to see. It was translucent and the effect was spreading up his arm. The pit of my stomach fell. He was fading away.

I pointed at him. "Please hurry. Something is wrong."

Zack's squinted up at Thomas's hand. "He doesn't belong there."

"But why is he vanishing?" Jimmy asked, crowding me at the mirror as he examined Thomas from head to toe.

"That's why. He isn't supposed to be there. It could take days or hours before he is gone completely, but it will happen. Time runs differently on their side." Zack waved us back. "Give me a little room, please."

My phone buzzed. I stepped a few feet back from Zack, tugging Jimmy with me as I stared at my phone screen.

Thomas: *Get out of there. He's coming.*

My heart jumped into my throat just as my phone dinged again.

Thomas: *I'm handcuffed in Thomas's car. This is Ash. Help me please.*

"We have to hurry," I said, my pulse drumming against my skull. "He is on his way into the hotel."

"Good." Zack rubbed his hands together, then pressed both palms against the mirror. "Release the living, bind the shadow. Release the living, bind the shadow. Release the living, bind the shadow."

Zack glanced at me, then over his shoulder just as Thomas stepped onto the landing. My hand tightened around Jimmy's and my other one reached into my pocket and encircled the stone cross. A wave of light zipped all around us as Zack began chanting again.

I slammed my eyes shut, focusing on the tiny grooves of the cross. The tips of my fingers twirled against the cool stone.

"What are you doing?" Thomas's voice thundered over me.

I gulped and squeezed my eyes tighter, listening intently to Zack's voice.

"Issa, look," Jimmy whispered in my ear.

I pried one eye open and peeked at the mirror. Thomas was brightening. I opened my other eye and glanced behind me. Thomas's body was frozen, a look of fury plastered on his face. The entity appeared as a dark fog gathering around Thomas as Zack's words slowly extracted him.

A guest door opened and an elderly man stepped into the hallway. He stopped short a few feet from Thomas and the apparition. He squinted, then blinked several times. Finally, shaking his head, he turned back to his room and went inside, shutting the door quietly behind him.

My held breath came out loudly and Zack jerked

from the noise. His gaze met mine and I shrugged apologetically.

The fog darkened as it moved away from Thomas's body, then another wave a light flashed from the mirror. I stepped back, watching as the half-man, half-skeleton reappeared on the other side of the mirror and then Thomas gasped in a lungful of air.

Jimmy raced over to Thomas and wrapped his arm around Thomas's waist to hold him steady. Thomas swayed as he drew in one long breath after another. I pressed my hand against his chest and smiled. He grinned in reply.

"Thank you, Issa," he breathed, leaning against the wall behind him.

"Super Issa, to the rescue." I winked at him, then turned back to Zack who was still sitting cross-legged in front of the mirror.

"I bind you to the mirror. I bind you from overtaking another body. I bind you from entering all portals."

My eyes narrowed. Rushing over to him, I kneeled down beside him. "If you bind him, how will he find his way to whatever comes next?"

"He lost that privilege," Zack muttered. His fingers trembled as he squeezed the rock hanging from his neck. "I bind you to the mirror. I bind you from overtaking another body. I bind you from entering all portals."

My gaze met the bloody woman's, who was now standing several yards behind the male apparition. The terror in her eyes spoke volumes.

"Who are you to make that call? And what about her?" I asked, grabbing Zack's arm. "How do we free her?"

"We don't. This portal is being shut down once and for all. All three will be barricaded in. And besides, this apparition is a slippery one. I can't lose the chance to bind him permanently to his side of reality." He ripped his arm from my grasp and continued chanting.

"No," I whispered, tears welling up in my eyes. She was here because of me.

I wiped at the tears furiously with the back of my fist, the stone cross still gripped firmly in the right one. Powerless to stop him, I watched as the woman silently screamed and the skeleton apparition flickered as he turned toward her with a wide smile lifting on his bony face.

"He's going to hurt her," I cried, squeezing Zack's leg and shaking him. "Stop. Please. We have to find a way to free her."

Zack quieted for a few seconds, but then shook his head and continued with his incantation, ignoring my pleas.

Both entities faded slightly. The grotesque, hunched-back ghost floated into view, once again. As he drew nearer, he blurred, then flickered like a candle, before vanishing completely. The skeleton apparition faded more, nearly disappearing completely, leaving only a pale silhouette still visible. Then the woman's eyes widened and she vigorously shook her head as her gaze snapped to Zack.

She stretched out her hand to him. Then her pleading eyes swept to me, before returning to the faded silhouette of the skeleton apparition. His hand snapped into view, pressing it hard against the mirror. It grew brighter than the overhead lights, illuminating down the hallway. The outline quivered for a few seconds, then he flashed and disappeared completely. The woman once again silently screamed, before vanishing into thin air as well.

The palms of my hands pushed against the glass. They were gone. Jimmy and Thomas stared at me through the mirror as Zack gathered his black rock, climbed to his feet, and stuffed the rock into his pocket.

"It was for the best," he whispered, shooting me a relieved look.

"She was innocent," I snapped, unable to stop the tears from streaming down my cheeks.

"She chose to not enter the light," Zack replied, wiping his hands across the front of his shirt. His fingers trailed down his chest muscles and he lifted his shirt as if he was examining it. Then a bright smile widened across his cheeks. "And I not only saved your friend, I cleaned up another one of your messes. How about a little gratitude?"

"Thank you, Zack." Thomas held out his hand to our

old tour guide. "I thought I was doomed to live my life in there."

Zack shook Thomas's hand, but as if he had been shocked, Thomas pulled back suddenly. He shook his arm, terror flashing across his expression. Backing away, Thomas sank to the first step of the staircase near the mirror and held his arm in his lap.

"Are you okay?" I asked him, forgetting to speak quietly.

Turning to me, Zack grinned and blocked my view of Thomas. "It is time to join the living, *Carissa*." He enunciated my name with a hint of malice, then winked. The glimmer in his eyes bit into my heart. For some reason, he was now enjoying our discomfort.

I glared at his receding back, grateful he was leaving and we now had our friend back. But a sadness was crushing my heart. Turning toward the mirror, I willed the woman to appear, even though in my heart I knew she was gone forever. And it was all my fault.

A whistle echoed down the corridor. My eyes lifted toward the sound, my skin prickling from its familiarity.

I turned to face Jimmy who was now sitting next to Thomas. His eyes were widening. My breath caught in my throat and I tried to suck in a breath, but it felt like the walls were closing in and suffocating me. Finally, gasping in some air, I couldn't stop myself from collapsing to my knees and weeping against the fabrics of the red carpet.

ACKNOWLEDGMENTS

Another story completed! I am so grateful for my family and friends who have listened to me talk about this supernatural tale and all the intricate pieces that fit it together. As always, it takes many to complete a book and this one was no exemption.

This story was originally published in Mischief Nights, a Halloween anthology published by Royalty Writes Enterprises. It was an absolute pleasure to work with that team. I always love the chance to step outside my usual genre and create something different, especially when the supernatural are involved. Thank you Royalty Writes Enterprises for the inclusion and all the hard work your team put in to make this publication seamless.

Thank you to my best friend and life partner, Steven, for encouraging me and loving me through the moments of uncertainty. You are a light in my life and I appreciate the space you hold for me.

I think my editor is the bomb! Seriously. She tells me like it is, no sugarcoating. I appreciate all her hard work and fantastic advice. Thank you, Angie for keeping my head on straight and holding me to a high standard with my writing.

To my dear friend Courtney, thank you for listening to me talk through my stories and writing on Marco Polo. Hours of listening to me yap away and you still aren't tired of hearing me! You are an amazing friend and supporter!

And as always, thank you from the bottom of my heart to all my readers! All of you make this possible. I am grateful that you love to hear from me, enjoy my stories, and support me on this journey! Thank you, thank you, thank you!

ABOUT THE AUTHOR

 International Bestselling Author Niki Livingston writes tales of epic and dystopian fantasy worlds filled with magic, mysticism, and mystery.

When she's not busy writing enchanting stories of diverse women rising in their power and strength, she spends her time walking her rescue puppy, quieting her mind with meditation and yoga, diving into the newest books of Veronica Roth and Anne Bishop, and binge-watching Game of Thrones, The Mandalorian, and The 100.

For all her latest releases and updates, subscribe to Niki Livingston's newsletter!

www.NikiLivingston.com